SPACE

For my grandson Ezra—just beginning the grand adventure of life—his big brother Luke, and all those who dare to walk the skies of their imaginations. —K. T. G.

For my daughter, Sasha, and my son, Kostya. —V. G.

STERLING CHILDREN'S BOOKS
New York

An Imprint of Sterling Publishing Co., Inc.
1166 Avenue of the Americas
New York, NY 10036

STERLING CHILDREN'S BOOKS and the distinctive Sterling Children's Books logo are registered trademarks of Sterling Publishing Co., Inc.

ISBN 978-1-4549-2099-1

Distributed in Canada by Sterling Publishing Co., Inc.
c/o Canadian Manda Group, 664 Annette Street
Toronto, Ontario, Canada M6S 2C8
Distributed in the United Kingdom by GMC Distribution Services
Castle Place, 166 High Street, Lewes, East Sussex, England BN7 1XU
Distributed in Australia by NewSouth Books
45 Beach Street, Coogee, NSW 2034, Australia

For information about custom editions, special sales, and premium and corporate purchases, please contact Sterling Special Sales at 800-805-5489 or specialsales@sterlingpublishing.com.

Manufactured in China

Lot #:
2 4 6 8 10 9 7 5 3 1
06/17
sterlingpublishing.com

The artwork for this book was created using ink and watercolor.
Design by Heather Kelly

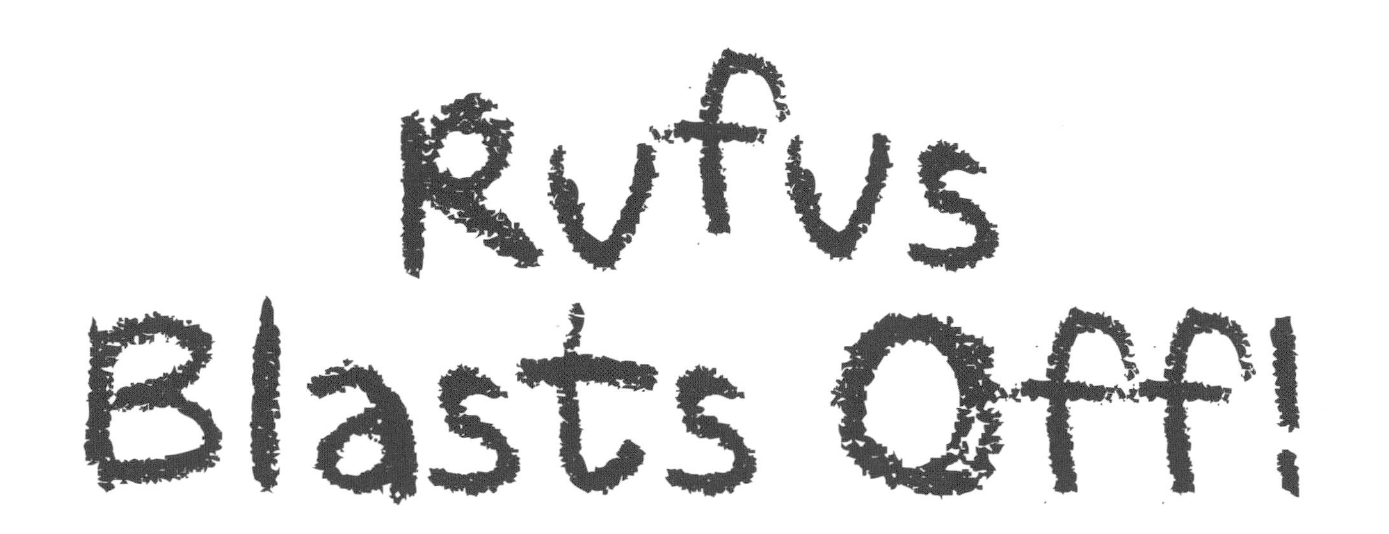

by
Kim T. Griswell

illustrated by
Valeri Gorbachev

STERLING CHILDREN'S BOOKS
New York

SCURVY
DOG

Rufus Leroy Williams III had a pirate's chest filled with books.

He loved every one.

And he read each book again and again . . . and again.

One day, Captain Wibblyshins wanted a new story.

"Arrrh!" said Rufus's pirate mates. "A *new* story!"

That night, Rufus climbed to the crow's nest.

He watched the Moon surf the waves.

He watched the stars wheel around the Moon.

He watched a red planet float far,
far above Earth.

Rufus knew just what to do. He would blast into space and find new stories.

But first, he needed a spaceship.

Rufus stuffed his gear into his backpack.

He grabbed his lunchbox and blanket.

Then he hopped into a skiff and rowed to shore.

"Good luck, piglet!" shouted Captain Wibblyshins.

Rufus slogged down the beach to the space center.

“My name is Rufus Leroy Williams III,” he said. “And I am ready to blast off.”

“This is the place!” said the guard.

The guard drove Rufus to the foot of a tall, tall elevator.

Up, up, up they zoomed. The guard rapped on the entry hatch.

"Commander Luna!" The guard saluted. "There's a pig to see you!"

"My name is Rufus Leroy Williams III," said Rufus. "And I am ready to blast off."

"No pigs in space," said Commander Luna.

"Why not?" asked Rufus.

"Because pigs draw smiley faces on the portholes," said Commander Luna.

"They do loop-the-loops in the crew cabin."

"They hog the juice packets."

"And they always want to push the buttons."

Rufus frowned. "But I brought treats!"

Commander Luna shook her head. "An astronaut needs the right stuff," she said. "And that's not it."

She marched Rufus back to the elevator.

Rufus Leroy Williams III really wanted
to blast into space. And he knew just what he needed.

"A space suit!"

Rufus rode the tall, tall elevator to the open hatch. He stepped inside and saluted.

"My name is Rufus Leroy Williams III," he said. "I am ready to blast off."

Commander Luna shook her head. "No pigs in space," she said.

"Why not?" asked Rufus.

"Because pigs pester the pilot," said the commander.

"They leave nose prints on the view screens."

"They forget to put the cap back on the toothpaste."

"And they *always* want to push the buttons."

"But I have a space suit," said Rufus.

"Still not the right stuff," said the commander, and she showed Rufus to the elevator.

Rufus Leroy Williams III really, *really* wanted to blast into space. And he knew just what he needed.

Rufus zipped up in the elevator and rapped on the hatch.

"Commander Luna!" Rufus waved his flag. "I'm ready!"

Commander Luna peered out the porthole.

"Nice flag," she said. "But not the right stuff to blast *this* bird into space."

"Why not?" asked Rufus.

Commander Luna sighed. “The mission is a no-go. Mission Specialist Rita was supposed to read a book live from Mars. Children all over the world were going to listen. But she has a cold and the doctor grounded her. The children will be so disappointed.”

“No they won’t,” said Rufus, and he held up his book. “I can read!”

“Specialist Williams, you *do* have the right stuff!” said Commander Luna.

"Welcome aboard! But be careful not to push any—"

A voice boomed through the cabin. "Ten, nine, eight . . ."

Rufus Leroy Williams III knew his numbers. He started counting down, too.

"Seven, six, five, four, three, two, one," Rufus counted. Then he frowned. "What comes next?"

"Blast-off!" shouted Commander Luna.

Within seconds they were high above the clouds.

The ship looped around Earth and shot into space.

It zoomed past a comet,

whipped around the Moon . . .

. . . and then slid to a stop at the space station.

“Load up for a long journey!” said Commander Luna.

When the ship was loaded, Commander Luna winked at Rufus.

"Go ahead, Specialist Williams," she said. "Push the button!"

The ship sailed through the starry deep.

It was a long . . . long . . . long . . . ride.

"Are we there yet?" Rufus asked the pilot.

"Patience, piglet," said the pilot.

"Are we there yet?" Rufus asked the science officer.

"Getting closer," said the science officer.

"Are we there yet?" Rufus asked Commander Luna.

"Naptime first!" she said. "And we'll be on Mars before you know it."

Rufus knew about naptime. He grabbed his blanket and a favorite book and snuggled in for a snooze.

When Rufus Leroy Williams III woke up, Mars filled the porthole.

"We're there!" he said.

Rufus bounced down the steps.

He did a back flip, a front flip, and a triple twist with a perfect landing.

Rufus Leroy Williams III loved the red planet.

He loved windsurfing.

He loved six-wheeling.

He loved Earth-gazing.

But Rufus loved reading most of all . . .

... because stories—old and new—are always best when shared with friends.

Rufus Leroy Williams III
READING FROM MARS
Rufus Blasts Off!
BREAKING NEWS:
WHEN PIGS FLY! LIVE WORLDWIDE BROADCAST!

Rufus
Blasts Off!
I ♡
reading!